Autobiographically inspired and dedicated to all nap-takers!
Thanks to Rachel with Olive, Sandra and Dagmar!

Ebenwald Verlag, Wattens, Austria
www.camel-o-shy.com
ISBN 978-3-90251-501-8

Sabine P. Moser has written & illustrated the following children books:
"A week with Camel-O-Shy", ISBN 3 902515 007
"Give it a try, Camel-O-Shy", ISBN 9 948853 857

Printed in Hongkong

EBENWALD

NO PROBLEM, CAMEL-O-SHY®!

This book belongs to

It was a quiet and
peaceful day in the desert —
Dubai wasn't very far away —

as Camel-O-Shy just finished
a nibble of his favourite tree,
and decided to take a nap
(as always from two until three).

He had just fallen asleep — well —
at least he had tried, when ...

"Hello, Camel-O-Shy!!"

a camel-boy's voice cried.

"I am bored and my mother is
out in the desert, you see.
She wants me to ask you whether
you would have time to play with me?"

"But first of all, before we start singing a song,
I'm taking my afternoon nap;
it doesn't take very long!

I always have a nap, from two until three,
so why don't you build a sandcastle in the
meantime and start ... without me?"

"No problem, no problem, you can have a camel-rest, no problem, I'll keep quiet and do my camel-best!...

But my mum always says I have to sleep "at night", and I thought what mum says is always, always right?"

"Yes, yes, that's right, but Camel-O-Boy, look at me!
Can't you see that my eyes are already closed so ...

PLEASE DON'T SPEAK TO ME!"

"Oh sure, no problem," whispered Camel-O-Boy,
"You can have your camel-sleep, don't worry,
I'll keep quiet now, you won't hear a peep!"

What's wrong —
there wasn't any noise?

"Why are you angry, I wasn't loud, don't
you agree? I only tried to pull you more into the
shade, but guess who's stronger, you or me?

But your eyes are now wide open —
so therefore I am allowed to speak?"

"No, no, my head is still sleepy and I'm beginning to feel sick:
no more questions, don't pull me, please let me rest,
if I don't sleep now, my food won't digest!"

„No problem, no problem,
you won't hear a peep."

So Camel-O-Shy tried again
to finally fall asleep.

But all of a
sudden a
sandstorm
appeared —
which was
quite unusual
for this time
of year.

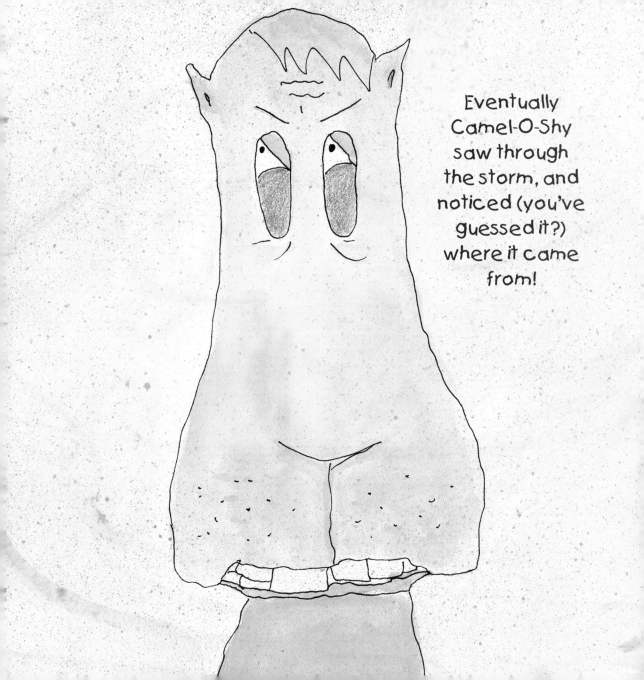

"But as you're awake now,
one last question ... maybe?
Look up! Don't you think the sun
moved — and is it almost three?"

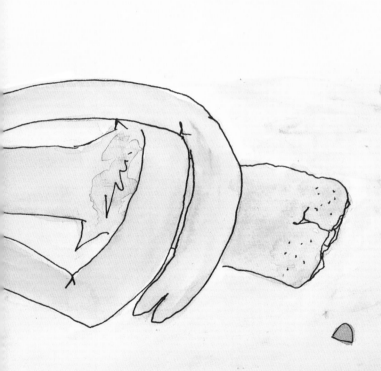
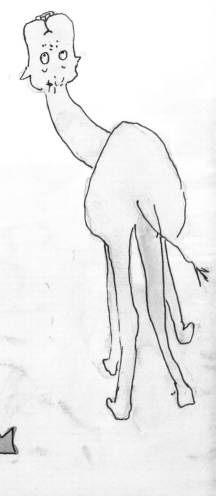

"No, definitely not, but you've convinced
me somehow, I'll soon get up and play,
I won't get much of a rest today,
not with you around me, anyway!"

"Just give me two more
minutes to finish my dream,
just stay here —
don't pull me,
no chasing, no screams!"

"No problem, no problem,
but you should have told
me so, NOW I will obey for
the two minutes to go."

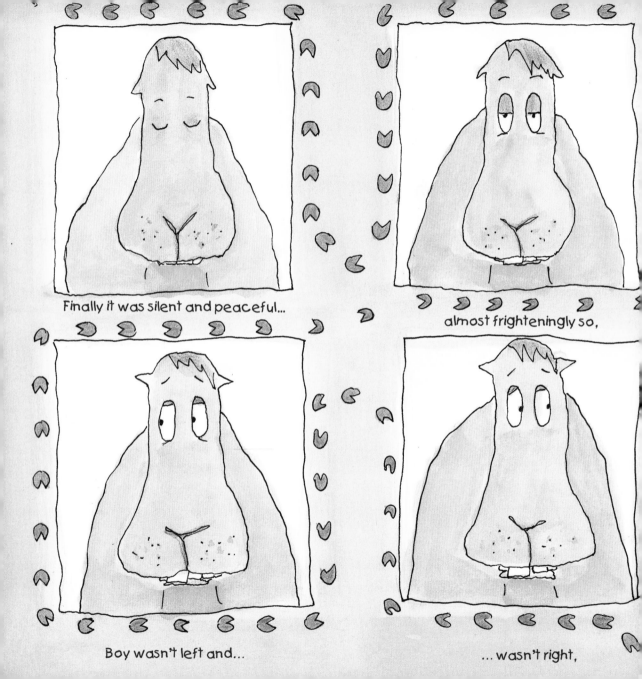

Finally it was silent and peaceful...

almost frighteningly so,

Boy wasn't left and...

... wasn't right,

where did he go?
He was completely
out of sight! When ...

"I'm up
here!!"

... a voice suddenly cried!

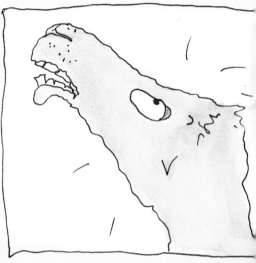

"I climbed up this high
tree all on my own!
Are the two minutes
over? Could you please
help me down?
Camel-O-Shy, I just don't
know what to do!
I think it's best
I let myself drop ...

... ON YOU!"

"Don't worry, Camel-O-Shy ...I'm fine.
I'm not hurt - so why the big sigh?

Well, after all this, I'M EXHAUSTED,
what about you, Camel-O-Shy?

Could you do me a favour,
I'm really tired, you see.

I must also have a rest now.
Could you wake me up at three?"

When Camel-Umm-Boy
came some time later —
imagine the surprise for
her to see, that both of
them were sleeping, and
it was way after three!

"What's your secret?", she whispered,
"Boy never keeps quiet when I want to rest.
What a perfect camel-sitter you are,
simply the best!"

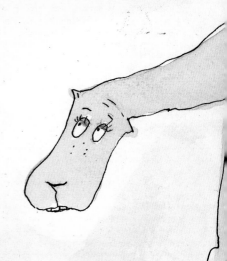

"Considering that, Camel-O-Shy,
I've got an idea ...
what would you say,
if I send Boy over now every day?"

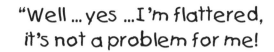

"Well ... yes ... I'm flattered,
it's not a problem for me!

But next time please,
could you send him at
QUARTER PAST THREE?"